W9-DBE-061

DATE DUE

DEMCO

Washington Irving's

RIP VAN WINKLE

retold by
Carol Beach York

illustrated by
Kinuko Craft

Folk Tales of America

Troll Associates

PROLOGUE

Most folk heroes have grown out of people's tall tales. Heroes like Paul Bunyan, John Henry, and Davy Crockett are bigger than life—able to do the most amazing things.

But Rip Van Winkle comes to us from a story written many years ago by Washington Irving.

Rip's name and his story are so well known that he has taken on the quality of a folk hero—although his only famous deed was *sleeping*. No daring acts. No life of adventure. Just sleeping.

But then, nobody ever slept like Rip Van Winkle!

Library of Congress # 79-66314
ISBN 0-89375-300-9/0-89375-299-1 (pb)

Rip Van Winkle lived in a small village near
the Hudson River, at the foot of the Catskill
Mountains. It was a long time ago, when wood
fires heated the little village houses and horses
trotted along the narrow village streets.
Weathervanes on the shingle roofs told the di-
rection of the wind.

Rip's village was founded by early Dutch set-
tlers. These people were sturdy and hard-
working. They built houses and kept them in
good repair. They planted potatoes and corn.
They mended their fences and weeded their
gardens.

But Rip Van Winkle wasn't much like them. Rip was a lazy, happy-go-lucky fellow who did as little work as possible—usually none. His cow strayed off, and his roof leaked. His plot of land was in sad shape, and getting worse every year.

But Rip never worried himself about such things. He would rather stroll through town with his dog, Wolf, than hoe corn or chop firewood. He took life easy. The village children tagged at his heels wherever he went, for Rip always had time to play marbles and fly kites with them.

"Tell us a story," the children would beg. And Rip always had time for that, too.

He would settle down with his back to a tree, and the children would gather around him, climbing in his lap and trying on his hat for fun. Ghost stories were his favorites. He also knew stories about witches and pirates. After he told one story, the children would tumble about, begging for another.

Everybody in the village thought Rip was a fine fellow. Everybody except his wife, Dame Van Winkle. She thought Rip was a lazy good-for-nothing. And she often told him so, at the top of her voice.

"Rip Van Winkle, you are a lazy good-for-nothing!"

You could hear Dame Van Winkle all the way to the schoolhouse when she really got going.

Sometimes she would throw a cooking pot at Wolf, just to show she meant business.

"Rip Van Winkle, the roof needs patching. Can't you put your mind to things?"

Rip liked to put his mind to things like fishing all day at the river. He liked to put his mind to things like tramping through the woods with Wolf, or hunting squirrels and rabbits in the mountain shrubbery. Actually, he never shot anything at all. But he always said he was going hunting just the same.

Dame Van Winkle was a plump, cherry-cheeked lady. Shouting at her husband made her face flush redder than ever. She got as dark as a plum. "Mend the roof *today!*" she would cry.

"It's going to rain," Rip would say, staring up at the sky—where there was not really a cloud to be seen for miles. "I can't mend the roof if it rains."

Rip was always good at excuses for not working. Dame Van Winkle would work herself
into a rage for nothing. But she kept doing it.

Even when Rip sneaked out of the house to
join his friends at the village inn, he wasn't safe
from her fussing. She would hunt him out, as
he sat with his friends on a bench under the
shade tree. It was all so lovely before she came.

Nicholas Vedder, the innkeeper, was always

there, puffing on his long pipe in the leafy shade. Van Bummel, the schoolteacher, always had the latest news to report. And any villager with a spare hour could be found there.

"See those birds flying South already? It's going to be a long winter."

The men on the inn bench would predict the weather, swap stories, take snoozes, and have a grand time.

Until Dame Van Winkle arrived.

"There you are, you loafer!" she would cry when she caught sight of Rip. "What will become of us! The cow is gone again, and the cabbage patch needs weeding, while you sit with your good-for-nothing friends!"

Rip would pretend not to hear. Dame Van
Winkle's face went from pink to dark red.
"You *idler!*" She would point a finger at
Nicholas Vedder, the innkeeper. "How can
you take care of your inn when you do nothing
but sit on this bench all day?"

It was a good question. Unfortunately, Vedder had no answer.

"You're a bad lot, all of you." Dame Van
Winkle went on and on. And on and on. It
spoiled the fun of going to the inn.

16

The only place Rip was really safe was in the woods. With his hunting gun over his shoulder, he would whistle for his dog, Wolf, and tramp off up the mountainside. Dame Van Winkle would have liked to track him down there—but *she* had work to do. There were children to care for, pots bubbling on the fire, and the cottage floor to sweep. Her chores were without end. She might go to the village inn to find Rip, but she didn't have time to chase after him when he went up the mountain.

And so it happened one day that Rip was scolded out of the house before breakfast. Then he was scolded off the bench at the inn before lunch. So he grabbed his gun, called his dog, and took flight to the woods.

It was a clear autumn day. The leaves were red and gold on the trees. It was a splendid day to do nothing but walk through the woods. Rip didn't catch any squirrels, of course, but he was having a good time. When he sat down to rest at last, the sun was low in the sky.

"Ah, Wolf," he said with some regret. "The sun is going down. It's time to start back if we want to get home before dark."

Wolf didn't look very happy about starting back home. Only that morning Dame Van Winkle had thrown a soup ladle at him. And then swept him out the door with her broom. He looked at his master with sad eyes.

And then a call came echoing through the woods.

"Rip Van Winkle! Rip Van Winkle!"

Rip and Wolf shuddered. Had Dame Van Winkle found them even here, far away in the woods?

"Rip Van Winkle!"

The call came again, and as Rip looked through the trees, a small man appeared. He was wearing old-fashioned clothes. He wore baggy breeches trimmed with buttons, and a wide-brimmed, sugar-loaf hat. He was a short fellow with long, heavy hair and a gray beard. And over his shoulder, he was carrying a wooden keg.

Rip did not know the strange man, but he was glad to see that it was *not* Dame Van Winkle. He hurried toward the stranger and offered to help him with the keg. The man said nothing as they went up the mountain, sharing the load of the wooden keg.

Wolf walked along behind.

18

Dusk was closing in. Although the sky was still fair, Rip heard the rumbling sound of thunder in the distance.

"Is a storm coming this fair day?" Rip said. But the little man did not answer.

The keg was heavy, and Rip was beginning to wonder how long they were going to carry it. Then they came to a flat, bare stretch of ground surrounded by trees. To his surprise, Rip saw that the noise he had thought was

thunder was coming from this place. In the
clearing, a group of small, bearded men were
bowling ninepins. The roll of the bowling balls
across the ground echoed like thunder up and
down the mountainside.

The men were dressed in the same old-style
clothes. There were buttons on their breeches,
feathers in their caps, and long knives hanging
from their belts.

They were a strange lot, with broad faces
and small eyes, thick beards and big noses.

21

All of them stared at Rip without a word.
They were not a very friendly group.

The keg that Rip had helped to carry was
filled with some sort of drink, which the little
men passed around. Rip had a glassful himself, and it tasted very good. When the players
went back to their game of ninepins, Rip
drank another glass.

The sun was gone now. Moonlight shone through the trees, lighting the faces of the little men. The game of ninepins went on. Nobody spoke to Rip or paid him any attention at all. He was left to himself and his empty glass.

"One more glass won't hurt," Rip told himself. "It's very tasty." He might have had a good many more, but he began to feel drowsy. It had been a long day, beginning with Dame Van Winkle's cry, "Out of bed, you lazy man!" Then a full afternoon of trudging through the woods.

"No wonder I'm tired," Rip murmured. And he fell fast asleep even with the roar of the ninepins game in his ears.

Wolf curled up his tail and lay down by his master. At least they were safe from flying pots and soup ladles. And the noise of the rolling balls was more soothing than Dame Van Winkle's voice.

When Rip woke up, it was morning. The sun was already high in the sky. Birds twittered in the trees, but otherwise the woods were still. The rumbling thunder of the ninepins game was gone. Indeed, Rip was back again in the place where he had sat down to rest before he saw the man with the wooden keg.

"How did I get back here?" Rip wondered. But right away there were more important things to wonder about.

His faithful dog, Wolf, was gone, and lying on the ground nearby was a rusty old gun.

"They've stolen my gun!" Rip exclaimed. "And my clothes!"

Now he was wearing a tattered, faded shirt and pants, and shoes that were full of holes.

And his beard had grown a foot long!

"Those scoundrels have robbed me *and* bewitched me!"

Rip scrambled to his feet.

"Wolf! Wolf!"

He called. He whistled. But no dog came bounding through the forest to him.

"My gun! My clothes! My dog!" Rip was fit to be tied, and he set off at once up the mountain toward the clearing where the men had been.

But, although he went up the mountain a long distance, he did not come upon the clearing.

"I've lost my way," he cried at last. The sun was going so fast across the sky that he dared not go much farther. Dame Van Winkle would be as mad as a hornet because he'd been gone all night. It seemed best to head for home.

But he did so with a heavy heart. He had been robbed of his dear dog and his gun, and left only with raggedy old clothes. Worse yet, a miserable scolding would be waiting for him.

No wonder he dreaded the first glimpse of his village.

But, as he approached the village, every-thing looked different! There were more houses than Rip remembered. There were houses he had never seen before. Rip thought he knew everyone in the village. He *did* know everyone in the village. Who were these strangers?

The children did not run up to him, begging for a story. They stared at him as if they did not know him. And, indeed, he did not know them.

Where was Betsy, the blacksmith's daughter?

Where was Jack?

Where was little Tom Brommer?

Rip did not see a familiar face among all the children. But they trailed after him, whispering

30

and laughing among themselves. Several dogs began to trot along beside the children, barking at Rip. Dame Van Winkle would not like all this, Rip was sure. But he went on down his own street, and at last he saw his own house.

But what had happened? The roof was sagging. The front door hung loose on its hinges. Shutters swayed and creaked at the windows. The yard was overgrown with weeds, and an air of gloom hung over the poor cottage.

The children gathered at the edge of the weed-grown garden, and the dogs sniffed about carefully as Rip went through the doorway. The house was empty! Dust and cobwebs lay thick on the floors and in the corners that Dame Van Winkle always kept so clean. No cooking pot or teakettle simmered at the fireplace. No little Van Winkles ran to greet their father. Rip called out their names, but silence echoed through the rooms.

Outside the dogs began to bark again, and
Rip went to the door in bewilderment.

"Wolf!" he called.

The dogs barked back and ran about in the
scraggly yard. But not one of them was Wolf.

With the children and dogs close behind
him, Rip rushed off toward the inn. His friend
Nicholas Vedder could tell him where his fam-
ily was.

But the inn was gone.

A new building stood on the spot. UNION HOTEL, the sign said.

And the shade tree was gone.

A tall pole stood in its place, and a flag hung at the top, waving in the breeze. Rip just stared at it. What flag was this? He had never seen it before. There were red and white stripes, and white stars on a blue background. Rip didn't recognize it at all!

At the doorway of the Union Hotel, a young man was passing out handbills to a cluster of people. He was talking to them about "liberty" and "elections." But when Rip appeared with his trail of children and dogs, the crowd at the hotel door forgot all their other business and gathered around him.

He was certainly a sight to see, with his rusty gun and ragged clothes and uncombed beard.

A stout, well-dressed gentleman pushed his way through the group and stood in front of Rip. Buckles on his shoes glistened in the sunlight, and he leaned on his cane in a grand manner.

"Why have you come to the election with a gun, old man?" the gentleman demanded. "We want no trouble here."

"My gun . . . why . . . it's only for hunting," Rip stammered.

"Some fine gun for hunting," a voice called from the crowd, and everybody laughed. Rip's rusty old flintlock was something to laugh about.

"We want no trouble here," the stout gentleman said again. He drew himself up importantly and frowned at Rip.

"A spy! He's a spy!" someone shouted. The crowd pushed in closer around Rip, and all the dogs began to bark.

"Quiet! Stand back!" the gentleman commanded. But it took a few minutes to get the people quiet again.

"Now, who are you, old man?"

Rip searched the crowd for a familiar face. "Where is Nicholas Vedder? He knows me. He can tell you I'll cause no trouble."

There was silence a moment, and then a white-haired man at the edge of the crowd spoke up.

"Nicholas Vedder? He's been dead eighteen years."

Rip's head was spinning. Nicholas Vedder dead eighteen years? How could this be?

"Van Bummel—the schoolmaster. He knows me."

"Van Bummel's gone," the old-timer at the edge of the crowd answered. "He went to the war. Now he's in Congress."

War? What war? Congress? It meant no more to Rip than the stars and stripes at the top of the flagpole.

"We'd better get that gun away from this old fellow," someone shouted. "He'll shoot it off and kill someone."

Rip was at his wit's end.

"Does no one know Rip Van Winkle?" he pleaded.

A kindly looking woman holding a baby stepped forward. "My father's name was Rip Van Winkle," she said. "But he's been gone twenty years. He went hunting one day and never came back."

"Twenty years?" Rip peered at the woman's face. It was his own little girl, Judith, grown up now and with a baby of her own. Tears came to his eyes.

"I am your father," he said in a trembling voice. "I am your father, Rip Van Winkle."

Then the whole crowd wanted to hear the story of his twenty years on the mountain. Who could make head or tail of it? Little men ... bowling on the mountain ... in the dead of night ...? The people began to wink at each other and tap their foreheads to show they thought Rip Van Winkle was crazy.

"Here comes Peter Vanderdonk!" someone called. "Let's ask him about this. He knows all the history of these parts."

A stooped old man was just then coming

along the road, minding his own business.
"What's all this commotion?" he cried as the
crowd drew around him. Everybody began
talking at once.

Then Rip had to tell his story all over again.
When he was finished, Peter Vanderdonk
nodded wisely.

"Aye, Rip," he said. "It's the ghosts of Hendrick Hudson and his crew you've seen. No
doubt about that. They put you to sleep for
twenty years."

"Hendrick Hudson?" Poor Rip did not know what to expect next.

"You've never heard of him?" Peter Vanderdonk put his face close to Rip's. "He discovered the Hudson River, you know. Oh, it's a long time ago. But he and his crew come back every twenty years just to keep an eye on things. It's them you've seen. Hudson and his crew. Ghosts. Dead these many years."

Some of the villagers still doubted. They whispered, "He's crazy. He made up the whole story."

Others in the crowd grew silent. Hadn't they heard the rumble of thunder in the mountains?

"Come home with me, Father," Judith said. She took his arm gently and led him through the crowd.

Rip lived with his daughter after that, and
his life was quite peaceful. Judith did not scold
and shout as Dame Van Winkle had done. Rip
was free to stroll about the village streets, or sit
on the bench by the Union Hotel. He missed
the shade tree, but otherwise he was very
happy there.

He had slept on the mountain not one night, but twenty years. He had missed the whole American Revolution! His country had fought for freedom against King George and England. And won.

"Tell us a story," the village children begged once again. And Rip Van Winkle was always ready, as before. Now his favorite story was his own, of course. Hadn't he always liked ghost stories best?

And whenever thunder rumbled in the mountains, Rip would say, "Listen! The little men are playing ninepins."

But he did not want to lose another twenty years. So he never went looking for the little men. It was better to sit on the bench and tell stories. Or take a snooze.

Sometimes in his dreams he heard Dame Van Winkle's voice again—"You lazy, good-for-nothing man!" But then he would waken. It was only a dream. Oh, joy. It was only a dream. Rip would puff on his pipe and look up at the clouds, soft and white above the Catskill Mountains, beside the Hudson River.